Maren's Hope

THE
LATTER-DAY DAUGHTERS
SERIES

Library of Congress Cataloging-in-Publication Data

Anderson, Launi K.,
Maren's Hope / by Launi K. Anderson
p. cm.
Summary: Maren helps a Mormon family care for their children, and
they help her to learn to read, but when her uncle forbids this contact,
Maren's hope is tested.
ISBN 1-56236-503-7
[1. Mormons--Fiction. 2. Frontier and pioneer life--Fiction.
3. Literacy--Fiction.] I. Title
PZ7.A54375Mar   1995
[Fic]--dc20   95-33437
                             CIP

10 9 8 7 6 5 4 3 2

Maren's Hope

THE
LATTER-DAY DAUGHTERS
SERIES

Launi K. Anderson

A S P E N
B O O K S

Dedication

*To Dane and Rhen, who will find their own Latter-day
Daughters some day. And to Devon, Daddy, and Andy,
with love.*

*I wish to thank my family
and Laurie, Lorie, Lynnette and Mom;
my best friends and most enthusiastic cheering section.
I love you.*

TABLE OF CONTENTS

Remember the worth of souls is great
in the sight of God.

D&C 18:10

CHAPTER ONE

A Price to Pay

The entry bell rang when we came through the door and scared us both half to death. Cecile grabbed onto my arm, took a deep breath, then let go. We were nervous enough just walking in this store. We didn't need any help feeling more jumpy. We came in behind an older lady so we could sneak to the back without being noticed.

Once we got inside, it was easy to forget what we came for. I closed my eyes and breathed in the warm smells. I could almost see Mama setting a fresh baked pie down in front of Papa himself. In my mind, Mama was beaming down at him and Papa had a big smile on his face.

This was a nice store. More friendly feeling than some others I'd been in.

A dozen candy jars sat in pretty rows on the countertop, and open baskets of crackers and potatoes lined the aisles. One barrel held a bundle of straw brooms and hickory rakes. Twisted hemp,* coiled up on the floor, looked like giant carriage springs. A large round of cheese, one wedge already missing, lay on a platter up front. I felt a gnawing ache in my stomach and made myself look away. A long row of lanterns hung from nails just above the front counter. I imagined them all lit up at once,  shining like a big spray of July fireworks. I was forced back from my daydream as Cecile yanked me down behind a pickle barrel.

"Maren, could you see it?" she whispered.

"No," I said, trying to keep my voice soft like hers. "Mama said cornmeal would probably be up behind the counter. We'll *have* to ask."

"We can't," she said. "What if he tells us it costs more than we've got?"

Cecile always liked to think the worst. If anything could be fretted over she'd get right to it. Not me.

Like Papa use to say, "I'd rather spit in the wind than whine over the storm." But Cecile says if I was fourteen like her instead of eleven, I'd know what there was to worry about in this world.

"What if he calls us beggars like the man at the last place?"

I clenched my teeth. Then glaring up at her, I said, "We're not beggars and this isn't the last place.

Our dresses are fresh scrubbed and . . . well look," I stuck my hand out, right up to her face, "even my fingernails are clean."

"I know, I know," she said. "But I'll just die if we don't have enough money again."

Just then a tall light-haired man found our hiding place. His eyes were as bright a blue as Mama's good dress used to be. At first he looked startled to see us. But then, smiling with a finger to his lips, he nodded, then reached for a pair of boots. He was pretending not to see us at all. We stood up straight and acted like we were needing some pickles.

I looked to where the clerk stood, wiping his hands on a crisp, white apron. He saw me. I wanted to duck back down but he called over, "May I help you ladies?"

I turned to Cecile, waiting for her to speak. Being older, it was her place; but she just stood frozen, like she'd seen a snake. I pushed past her and marched up to the counter. The clerk looked like a kind enough man, but you can never really tell about store clerks. Some smile all helpful-like, until they find out you don't have enough money. Then mostly they won't talk at all. Last time was the worst.

Cecile did the talking back then, while four-year-old Phillipe hid behind my skirt. We were hoping to buy some flour, just a pinch, when the store lady said, "Hey, you there! How much money you got?" We showed her our two pennies, and she started laughing. Not a happy laugh, but a mean one. Next thing we knew she was throwing potatoes and screaming, "Get out! Filthy beggars. I'll have the constable after you."

We'd scattered like field mice, then doubled back and picked up all the broken potatoes.

Cecile said, "It isn't really stealing 'cause the lady threw them to us, didn't she? No one buys split potatoes anyway." I couldn't help thinking, we never had this trouble before. I sure do miss my Papa.

Now, the clerk asked again, "Can I help you?"

I could see it was time for me to do the talking.

"Yes sir. We just came in to check the price of your cornmeal. Our Mama says she'll come back later to buy ten, maybe twenty pounds." I heard Cecile gasp behind me and knew she had her hand over her mouth, the way she always does when I'm making things up. But I didn't flinch. "For now, how much is it for just one pound?"

The clerk smiled and stepped aside saying, "I'm sorry, Miss. I didn't realize I was blocking the signs. Everything is marked here behind the counter. Let me know if you need anything." He walked back to talk to the man by the boots. They acted like they were already friends.

My heart started pounding and a warm flush came over me. The black writing on the signs looked like beautiful swirls and squiggles. Nothing else.

"Now what do we do?" Cecile said. She sounded like she was going to cry. "Which one says corn-meal?"

"I don't know," I said.

There wasn't a real school to go to back in Colburn. A lot of folks taught their children at home, but that didn't work for us. Papa never had much book learning himself; not enough to teach us, anyway. Mama tried the best she could, but her upbringing is French-Canadian. Sometimes English is hard enough for her to speak. She can't read or write it, so neither can we.

Now, coming all this way from Canada left us looking like ragged poor folk. But I figure, maybe that's what we are.

"Well ladies? Was there something else?" The clerk was back.

"No thank you," Cecile said, pulling my arm.

I pulled back. "Let go of me," I said. Then, try-ing to look like I knew what I was doing, I said, "Yes sir, there is. We would like a small bag of cornmeal."

"Fine enough," he said. "Five pounds of corn-meal."

"Wait," I said. "Mother will want just a small bit

for starters. Could we try say, one pound?"

The man looked puzzled but nodded, "Of course, miss. I'll just weigh you out some." He turned to his scale and set the small disc weight* down on one side and began pouring a tiny amount of meal into the bowl at the other end.

"Thank you," I said. Turning back to Cecile I motioned to her to cross her fingers.

She took the three pennies out of her pocket and without saying anything tucked my fingers around them. In my mind I chanted, "Three cents, three cents, three cents." Cecile stood quiet, chewing her lip.

The merchant shook down the cupful of meal, folded the bag and tied a string around it. He winked at me as he slid the sack across the counter. The hair was sticking to the back of my neck and suddenly the air in the store felt dry and hot.

"That will be five cents, please."

I closed my eyes and gulped hard. Suddenly a dull thud behind me sent the merchant running to my side. Without turning, I knew. Cecile had fainted again.

"I'm sorry, to cause all this fuss," I said. The clerk propped Cecile's head up on a small sack of grain. Kneeling at her side I whispered, "Would you please wake up."

I tried to calm down the poor clerk by telling him that Cecile did this at least once a week.

"Really sir, we hardly notice anymore. We all just wait a few minutes and she turns up fine." It didn't seem to make him feel any better. He sat patting my sister's hand saying, "Miss, are you all right?" Finally, he disappeared into the back to get some water.

I put my hand under Cecile's neck and pulled her hard till she was nearly in my lap.

"You are embarrassing me!" I said, giving her arm a shake. She began to stir and tried to sit up.

The boot man came down the aisle and didn't see her all sprawled out on the floor until he nearly fell over her.

"Oh dear," he said, "has she been hurt?"

"No sir, Mama says she's just got thin blood."

He pulled out a handkerchief. Then, taking the cup from the clerk's shaky hand, he poured a little water onto it and laid it gently on Cecile's forehead. With a playful glint in his eye, he looked up and said, "Well, Newel, are your prices so high now that the ladies are swooning?"

"Truly, Joseph, she fell to the floor, just like that,"

Newell said, snapping his fingers. "No warning whatsoever. Perhaps it's too hot in here. Maybe I should let the fire die down."

"Nonsense. There is nothing wrong with your fire. It feels wonderful," Joseph said. I stuck my fingers into the cup and flicked water right in Cecile's face. She opened her eyes wide and sat straight up.

"Let's get out of here," I said pulling her to her feet.

"Hold on now," Joseph said. "Are you sure she's feeling well enough to walk?"

Cecile hung her head down and said, "I'm fine, sir. Thank you."

"You're certain?"

I smiled weakly. "She'll be fine." I wondered why he was so worried about us. With my arm tight around Cecile's waist, I helped her to the door. We started through, and she stumbled a bit. In a second, both men were at our sides again. Newell wanted to find the doctor. Joseph reached over a barrel of nails and lifted up a bench for Cecile to sit on.

"Listen," Joseph said, "my wagon is right outside. I'd be honored to take you home. Your sister doesn't seem steady enough yet to walk."

I just looked at him for a minute. The afternoon was getting colder and my feet did ache from coming through the frozen fields of corn stubble. My shoes were wet and rattled with the pebbles that had sifted in. It would be so fine to ride home in a wagon.

I remembered coming to town with Papa, way back. I could almost see the way the sun shone down on his brown hair, making it look nearly yellow. Sometimes if I closed my eyes and thought real hard I could hear Papa singing while he held the reins. Papa was a terrible singer but we didn't care. It always made us laugh.

Now, it had been nearly two years since Papa took sick with the ague. There wasn't any doctor around and we couldn't tell exactly what to do. Papa lay shivering, like he was freezing, for three days. Then he was just real still and quiet. On the fourth day, he died. Even though I was right there to see it all, sometimes I still find myself looking up the road, hoping to see him coming home.

Papa never even saw the new baby that was born two days before Christmas. My brother Ren had gone looking for dry wood so we could have a fire. The baby came before he got back. Cecile wrapped her up in a clean flour sack while she was still warm and steamy. We all snuggled up around her. She had lots of black hair like the rest of us, and Papa's dark eyes. Now and then, Mama would cry when she held her, saying, "*Ma pauvre petite choute.*"* I guessed she was missing Papa for herself and the baby now. We named our new one Faith Noelle Saunders.

Now, Cecile was tapping on my arm. "Maren, we need to go."

"Let's take the ride," I said, surprised at my own words. We were new in Kirtland and it would be good to finally say we knew someone. Someone besides Aunt Elizabeth, that is. Anyway, there was something about this man, something kind and safe. He reminded me of Papa so I couldn't help liking him.

"You know we can't," she said, her lips barely moving. "What would Mama say?"

"I don't know, only my feet hurt. I can hardly walk myself, never mind pull you along. Anyway, you shouldn't worry so much!"

"On my honor, ma'am," Joseph said, "I give you my word. Straight home, no dawdling. Just point the way." He opened the door with a flourish and gestured for us to go through. I wrinkled my nose at Cecile and walked out.

This Joseph was a large man. And broad enough, I'd say, to wrestle down a bear. Though somehow I got the feeling he was the kind of man who would end up not fighting at all and march away friends. There was something about his eyes I couldn't quite make out. Whatever it was, it made me feel all hushed inside. Mama always says you can read a man's soul in his eyes.

Cecile huffed and gave me the "you're really gonna' get it" look, then stalked out the door.

Turning to Newell, Joseph said, "My friend, it wouldn't do to forget Emma's list." He pulled a torn piece of foolscap* from his coat pocket and read, "We'll need five pounds of salt, two dozen eggs, a quart of molasses, ten pounds of sugar, and twenty pounds of cornmeal."

Cornmeal. That word again. My ears perked at the sound of it, but I felt angry thinking of all the trouble it had caused and how sad Mama would be when we came home without it.

"And Newel," Joseph continued, "I believe I will take the boots. That trip to Missouri certainly took its toll my feet. I have strict instructions from Emma to get whatever shoes are necessary to keep my stockings out of her mending basket." At this, both men laughed. I stood quiet feeling the cold floorboards through the hole in my own shoe.

CHAPTER TWO

The Wagon Ride

I didn't think I had much to say, so it would have suited me just fine to ride the two miles to our place in silence. But our driver was not the quiet type. I didn't mind listening to his calm, pleasant whistling. It took my mind somewhere besides Cecile's scowl and the fact that she was right. Mama wouldn't be happy.

We bumped along over the frozen, rutted roads leading past the inn and over the bridge. Riding around the field instead of through it made it a longer way home.

He seemed to know everyone in town, for his hand waved high over his head at nearly every person we passed. People shouted from windows, fields, and porches, "Hey there, Brother Joseph," or "Good afternoon, Brother Joseph." Finally, when I couldn't stand it another second, I said, "Are all these people kin of yours?"

Cecile nudged me hard with her leg, but "Brother Joseph" just tossed his head back and laughed.

"Well now," he said, "let me think about that for a moment. I suppose one could say we are all family, true enough, though not directly related." I didn't know what he meant, but he went on. He said that many of the folks around here belonged to the same church and that everyone called everyone else Brother this, and Sister that. Then he asked the particulars of everyone in our family. Cecile frowned the whole time, but I didn't care. I liked talking to someone who didn't notice I was only eleven.

"We just came here, all six of us, from Colborn last month," I said. "That's in Canada. Our Aunt Elizabeth sent every penny she had to bring us here. With Uncle Riley away, for who knows how long, she was feeling the need of company."

Truth was, no one had a clue where Uncle Riley was. He rode off on his gray mare to go hunting one day and didn't come back. Aunt Elizabeth didn't fret over it much though. She was a sturdy woman and never liked being looked after anyway. "Besides," she said, "he was an ornery old thing." I hoped down deep that he'd come back. Him being my Papa's only brother, I figured just having him nearby would ease the ache a bit.

"So your family lives with Elizabeth Saunders?" Joseph asked. "I didn't know she had that big of a place."

"Oh, she doesn't. Not big enough for two mice, I'd say. It's cozy all right, but we manage. She says if we're gonna freeze to death or starve, we'd just as well do it as a family."

"Maren, please!" Cecile said. Her face was red and she looked so embarrassed. I shouldn't have said anything about starving. Everyone always tells me to think before I talk. But sometimes I forget.

Joseph stared down at me sadly, the reigns going limp in his hands. I looked straight ahead and tried to think of something to say. But he beat me to it.

"Maren," he said, casually, "you haven't told me about your father."

Cecile sat up straight, her eyes real big.

"Well, sir," I said slowly, "our Papa is out of town, right now." Cecile covered her face with her hands. I don't know what made me say it exactly. There is no shame in having a dead papa. But I don't like people always feeling sorry for us.

"I see," he said, looking off at the fields of corn stubble as we passed. "Well this is just wonderful!"

"It is?" I asked, surprised.

"Yes. I've been meaning to look in on Sister

Saunders for some time. And now, perhaps I can meet her family as well."

Without a warning Cecile spoke up louder than her usual self. Looking straight at me she said, "No, sir. That wouldn't be possible. Our mama's real busy, and she doesn't take to strangers. And anyway, it's nearly dinnertime." She said the last few words through her teeth so I could tell she was real mad.

"Yes, of course you're right," he said. We pulled up to the young willow tree which sheltered Aunt Elizabeth's tiny home. A tiny stream of black smoke curled out of the hole in one side of the roof. Aunt Elizabeth and Mama would be inside getting dinner. Without the cornmeal, there wouldn't be much.

Joseph pulled the horses to a halt outside the fence and jumped down. He lifted us both to the ground, one at a time. He was gentle, like he was afraid he'd hurt us. Cecile managed a curt "Thank you," then walked toward the house.

He took my hand and shook it lightly. "It's been a pleasure meeting you, Maren." His smile made me feel I'd known him forever. I couldn't help grinning. "Tell your Aunt Elizabeth that Emma and I will look in on her soon."

"I will, sir," I said, running toward the house. I slowed my step some realizing that I wasn't anxious to open the door.

As I came in, everyone was quiet and still, staring at me. Finally Mama spoke, her voice sounding strained and tired. "Maren, I've been so worried. Phillipe has been watching the field. Why were you so long?"

Cecile stood, looking all prim, offering no help with my explanation. Aunt Elizabeth sat quietly in the old birch rocker, holding the baby.

"Mama," I said, "we didn't come home straight through the field. We went way around it, on the road. I'm sorry to make you worry." She just kept looking at me. "Cecile wasn't feeling well, and . . ." Cecile's eyes narrowed at my attempt to blame our lateness on her. "Mama, don't be angry. We got a ride from the store."

Mama's eyes looked fearful and she reached over, taking me by the shoulders. "A ride?" she said. "A ride with who?" Not waiting for me to answer, she said, "Maren, we don't know anyone here! I've told you not ever to speak to people we don't know." Mama is a very gentle woman. There have only been a few times I remember hearing her raise her voice. It was only when one of us was in some kind of danger. I felt shameful at causing her more worry. I looked at the floor and said, "I'm sorry, Mama."

Chewing my lip to keep from crying, I glanced up at Cecile. Her face softened a little and she said,

"Don't be angry with Maren, Mama. It was my fault." I stared at her and felt like it was my turn to faint. "I had one of my spells again, and wasn't sure I'd make it home."

"But, Cecile . . ." Mama said, shaking her head.

"He's a nice man," I said. "Everyone in town must know him. They call him Brother Joseph."

Hearing this, Aunt Elizabeth looked up, a wide smile spreading across her face. "Brother Joseph?" she asked.

Cecile looked over at me then back to Aunt Elizabeth. We nodded.

Aunt Elizabeth set Noelle on the floor and got up from her chair. With a look of perfect delight on her face, she said, "It's all right, Marguarite. The girls couldn't have been in safer company."

She went to the door and pulled it open. Mama went to her side. She seemed confused but said nothing. They both looked out into the twilight at the wagon growing smaller and smaller as it rumbled down the road.

"He is one of the reasons I brought you here to Kirtland." Aunt Elizabeth slipped her arm around Mama's waist. We all crowded into the doorway, Cecile and I looking first at each other and then at our Mama. She stood with her head rested on Aunt Elizabeth's shoulder. Cecile nudged me and pointed out to the first fence post. There, stacked in a sturdy pile, was the cornmeal, the salt, the eggs, and even the sugar. All the supplies he'd purchased for his own family.

"That, my dears," Aunt Elizabeth said softly, "is Joseph Smith, the Prophet."

CHAPTER THREE

Man of the Family

Phillipe pranced around the room like a spring pony.

"Hold still," Cecile said, pulling the nightshirt over his head on one of his passes by her.

"Now Mama, now?" he said.

"Not yet son. Soon," Mama said calmly.

Every night, as the little ones were being snuggled into bed, Aunt Elizabeth told us the stories of the gospel that was stirring all around this town. She started out slow, about a week or so after we arrived, but now . . . we came to wait for the evening like horses thirsty for water.

We learned about the young boy who prayed to know which church to join and ended up seeing God himself and Jesus, too. Later, that same boy was given a kind of golden bible which the Lord helped him read. He wrote it down and now it was called the Book of Mormon. Cecile and I were struck with wonder to learn that this same boy was the man we rode home with, weeks ago. Aunt Elizabeth said he was a prophet of God, and we believed her.

A while back, she took all of us over to Isaac Morley's house for church services. We were scared to death. Our clothes were old and shabby, and little Phillipe had no shoes at all.

To our surprise, we were greeted with smiles and handshakes and gathered in like long lost family. Father Morley showed us his own copy of the Book of Mormon and even let me hold it. I was so filled with peace while it was in my hands that I almost started crying. Nothing had ever made me feel like that before. It was like a heartache, only good.

I wished Papa could have met these folks. They all seemed so happy, and I know he would have taken to them.

One Sunday when it was warmer than it should have been, we met outside in the meadow. There were twice as many Saints at this particular meeting. Before long we saw why. There, standing behind a makeshift pulpit* with a look of pure joy on his face, stood the Prophet Joseph. The entire time he spoke I tried not to gawk at him, but it was hard. He had such a kindness about him. After a few minutes, he looked at me. Right into my face. Then he smiled. I think he remembered me.

Phillipe's pleading brought me back. "Can we

hear our stories now, Aunt Elizabeth?"

"It won't be long, dear," she said. "We should wait for Ren."

I smiled to myself remembering that this was the day. Ren, my sixteen-year-old brother, had been gone nearly a week. He'd been working as a farmhand at the Simons' place, and tonight he would be home.

We were always anxious to see what Ren would come back with, 'cause so many folks hereabouts pay their help in kind.*

A while back, he found work as a splitter in a chair shop. He was given three chairs for his week's pay.

Last week, he was given a rooster and two hens for helping an older couple set a new roof before the snow came down hard. We named them Hickory, Smoke, and Chester, and planned from the start to let them stay as set-ting hens, until we had a yard full of chicks.

Then one day not long after our wagon ride from the Whitney store, we found a basket filled with apples, right outside the house. We couldn't think of where it had come from. Later, a small barrel of flour was left. This very morning we discovered a wrapped slab of bacon leaning up against the front door.

21

Cecile and I were sure that Brother Joseph was the reason our tummies were full these days. Aunt Elizabeth assured us that he couldn't possibly be doing it. She said he lived a day's ride away, in Hiram—more than thirty miles off. All I know is, that even without Papa, the world sure feels like a better place when my stomach isn't sore and empty.

Suddenly, the door banged open. There stood Ren with a tired smile, stomping the mud off his feet.

"Gracious, boy," Mama said, making her way to him. "You needn't break the door down."

"Sorry, Mama," he said winking over at us. "It's just so cold outside, I thought maybe it would be frozen shut." We giggled.

Mama tried to look stern, then gave up and laughed along with the rest of us. When Ren hugged her, her feet came right up off the floor.

Phillipe said, "What'd you bring us?" as he bounded across the room. Ren caught him under the arms and swung him up and over his shoulder.

"Bring you?" he said. "Was I supposed to bring you something?"

Phillipe slid down from his shoulder and shuffled, head low to Mama's side.

"Ren," Mama said.

"Wait now," Ren said, "I do have something

here." He pulled a small brown wad of paper from his pocket and tossed it to Phillipe.

It took him three seconds to tear it open. "Maple!" he said.

Ren ruffled Phillipe's hair. "Share that now, won't you?"

"Yes, sir!" he said, looking for a way to break up the sugar lump.

Ren gave us each a hug. He scooped up Noelle and kissed her forehead.

Mama set a bowl of bread pudding and apple-sauce on the table and took the baby from him. "Come now. Sit. Eat. We all want to hear how your week went."

"Maren," Ren said, "fetch the parcel out on the porch for me. Mrs. Simons sent over a mound of butter. That's one thing they have plenty of."

Settling back in his chair, he said, "Well, Mama, my week went real good. The weather held and some days we worked right through, past dark. When we finished the calving shed, we added on to the barn. Mr. Simons was so pleased with the work that he paid me like a regular hand."* Then with a grin, he opened a small bag of coins making sure it jingled loud enough for everyone to hear. Mama stared as he poured the coins into her hands. "It's only about a dollar, Mama, but it'll help some. Mr. Simons said if you can spare me, he can use me permanent."

Mama gasped. "How wonderful! Ren, jobs are so hard to find now. Did he say what you'll earn?"

"Here's the deal," he said. "The Simons are more or less like everyone else flooding into Kirtland. Plenty of work to do. Short on money. But he says he can come up with twenty cents a day."

"So much?" Mama said, shaking her head in amazement.

"It's the regular wage for hired hands," Ren said. "But he offered me another choice. He says he could give me five cents a day and meals. Then, if I work steady, come spring, he'll let me single out a milk cow and keep her first calf. What do you say, Mama? It will still be hard going for a while, but think of it. Our own cow!"

She was speechless, shaking her head as if she didn't believe a word he was saying.

My mind raced. I could see it all now. Milk. Butter. Cheese. Cream. I closed my eyes and saw myself selling all these things in town in exchange for everything we had ever wanted. Shoes, blankets, Sunday clothes, horses, a buggy. Before I could stop myself, I blurted out, "We'll be rich!"

Everyone turned and looked at me. Then a roar of laughter shook the room. I felt my face turning red as Ren came over and knelt down by my side. He tugged at my black braid and said, "Well, not rich just yet. But things *are* looking up a bit. Mr. Simons also says I can use his tools to work around here as long as I bring them back each morning. What do you think, Mama?"

From where Mama was sitting, I could see her face glowing in the lamplight as she watched her boy with pride. She nodded.

Aunt Elizabeth got up now and crossed the room. With her hand on his shoulder, she said, "Ren, it's so good of you to take care of all of us this way. With the Lord's help and yours, we may just make it, after all."

CHAPTER FOUR

House Guests

Aunt Elizabeth's sod hut* was nestled into a wooded corner of the Morley farm, about ten minutes away from the big house.* It was plainly thrown together to fit two people. When Uncle Riley left last

year the house was cozy enough for Aunt Elizabeth alone. We were hoping to make do till spring, but with the cold driving us inside more and more, her house needed stretching.

Now, with one of the last clear days we thought we'd see in a long while, Ren was frantic to get the sod cut and built up as an extra room before the ground froze solid and the sky turned black. It was slow going, and after three hours the back wall was not even a foot high.

"Wish I was a boy," I mumbled.

Ren blew breath out and frowned at me. "Why would you say that?"

"If I was a boy, Mama wouldn't say nothing about the both of us cutting sod. I could heave it around as good as you." I sat with my chin in my hands feeling sorry for myself. "If I was a boy, no one would say 'keep out of the way.' Then maybe I could be some real help."

Ren took out his handkerchief and mopped at his brow. He nudged me over and sat down by my side on the stump. A cool breeze flew past us, and Ren put his head back to let it blow through his hair. Then patting my leg he said, "Well, girl or not, I don't know what I'd do without you." Looking off to the northern sky he said, "I get the feeling this sunshine isn't going to last long enough."

Suddenly we heard the sound of a wagon pulling up in front of the house. We came around the corner in time to see a man in a gray waistcoat* handing a baby down to a beautiful lady with black hair like Mama's. She wore a ruffly dark blue dress, edged with creamy white lace. The sleeping baby on her shoulder had a head of white curly hair. The lady looked across the yard at me and smiled.

As the man turned, I saw that he was holding another baby with blonde curls, also asleep in his arms. As he faced the sunlight, I said, "It's Brother Joseph."

"Well, I'll be," Ren said. He rubbed at the dirt on his palms, keeping his eyes on the family now walking in our direction. "Maren, run and tell Aunt Elizabeth she's got visitors." He looked at me staring and said, "Maren, go!"

Startled out of my trance, I ran into the house.

"Mama! Mama!" I said, as fast as I could, "Brother Joseph is here with his wife. She's beautiful. And they have two babies!"

Mama quickly reached up and touched her hair, making sure it was in place. She untied her apron and tossed it over a chair.

"Phillipe, fetch Aunt Elizabeth. She's out gathering eggs. Cecile, finish giving Noelle her breakfast." Turning to me she said, "Well, open the door, Maren."

"Yes, Mama," I said, giving the door a yank. There, on the porch, stood the lady with her hand in the air ready to knock. Seeing me her eyes opened big. She smiled and dropped her hand to her side. Mama came up next to me and we all stared at each other for a minute.

"Hello," the lady said. "My name is Emma Smith. It seems my husband, Joseph, has disappeared around back with your son."

Mama smiled. "I'm pleased to meet you. Won't you come in?"

As Sister Smith came into our dark, simple home it struck me how out of place she looked. But she certainly made the room seem brighter.

The baby in her arms looked troubled at being in a home different than his own. I wanted to hold him real bad, but I didn't dare ask.

Just then Aunt Elizabeth came in. She set down her basket of eggs and hugged Sister Smith as Mama pulled up a chair for her. We propped the door open with a bucket so the light could pour in, and the ladies started talking.

I made up my mind to make friends with this baby. I couldn't really tell how old he was—him being bundled up and all. But he seemed a bit younger than Noelle, who was walking already. Scooting my chair over I started making silly faces at him. Finally, I mustered up enough courage to ask, "What do you call him?"

Sister Smith turned and said, "His name is Joseph. And isn't he happy with you? Why, usually he just clings to me and buries his face at the least bit of attention. He is so shy. Now his sister on the other hand . . ."

That's right I thought. Twins. Aunt Elizabeth told us about the babies. She said that Sister Smith had given birth to two small babies back last spring but they both died the same day. Then a man named John Murdock came and asked the Smiths to care for his twin babies, seeing as how his wife had taken ill and died. He let the Smiths keep the babies for their very own.

From outside the door we could hear men's laughter. We looked up to see Brother Joseph coming through the door, his arm around Ren, the other arm still holding the baby girl.

Brother Joseph was nearly a head taller than Ren. The dark brown of Ren's eyes was more striking next to Brother Joseph's bright blue ones.

They stopped laughing as they realized we were all staring at them. Brother Joseph said, "Emma, this young man is adding to this house, alone. He is both cutting and throwing the sod. I shook his hand, and I'll tell you he's as strong as an ox!"

In two strides he was beside Aunt Elizabeth, clasping her hand in his. "And how are you, Sister Saunders?"

"We're fine, Brother Joseph. What brings you here?"

"When I saw you at services last week, Emma reminded me that we'd not yet met your family. Though," he said, shooting a playful look in our direction, "a couple of them look rather familiar." Cecile and I began to giggle.

Mama had us fetch the johnnycakes* from the cupboard, while Aunt Elizabeth introduced everyone. Brother Joseph shook each hand and smiled, saying a few kind words to each of us in turn. Looking more serious, he said, "Is there any word yet from your husband, Sister Saunders?"

"No," Aunt Elizabeth said, "But after all this time, I really don't expect the news to be good."

"I'm so sorry," he said.

We sat listening to them talk for nearly an hour. Then Brother Joseph stood and said, "Emma, I'd like to ride back to the big house and talk to Father Morley."

I was disappointed to think he was about to leave. "Will Emma be all right here for a while?" he asked.

Mama and Aunt Elizabeth both said, "Of course," at the same time.

Then, turning to me he said, "Maren, would you mind keeping an eye on Julia? I'll be about an hour."

My mouth dropped open and my head nodded. Mama smiled as he bent low and gently placed the child in my lap. She was a beautiful little thing. All rosy-cheeked from sleeping. Her brother gurgled at me now, as if holding his sister made me "all right."

Leaning down, he kissed his wife on the cheek and touched the baby's hair. "I'll be back as soon as I can."

I don't know how long Brother Joseph was gone, but I was in heaven. One baby on my lap and another making eyes at me.

"Maren," Emma said, "little Joseph is taken with

you! I wonder . . ." She paused thoughtfully. "You see, we are living with a very kind family in Hiram named the Johnsons. Their children are all grown, and with Joseph away so much of the time, well, there is often more to do than I can manage. We've talked many times of hiring someone to help us. And now seeing Maren with the children . . . Mrs. Saunders, would you consider allowing her to come back with us?"

Mama sat looking blankly at Sister Emma. For a moment the silence was uncomfortable.

"Mrs. Saunders," Emma said, "I haven't offended you have I?"

"Oh no, no," Mama said, shaking her head. "It's just that, I guess I hadn't noticed how quickly my girls are growing up."

"She could ride back home as often as Joseph comes to Kirtland, which is at least every month or so. We could pay her in supplies," she smiled. "Money is scarce these days."

I chewed my thumbnail in silence, watching Mama's face. Part of me felt excited thinking of such an adventure. But then, looking around the room, at my family, the faces I loved, I wanted to shout, "No! I can't leave."

Mama nodded her head slowly. "This is good," she said. "Maren is young, but very strong. Of course, it must be for her to decide."

"What do you say, Maren?" Emma said gently. "Would you like to come live with us?"

I gulped hard. Looking into Mama's eyes, I knew how much the extra food and supplies would help our family. But I didn't want to leave.

Mama arose and came over to my side. She stooped down, taking my hand in hers. "Don't be frightened, *ma petite lapin*.* Can you do this for awhile? If it makes you sad or lonely, they will bring you home to us."

"You have my word," Emma said.

Then taking my chin, Mama whispered, "You are a lucky girl. How many can say they have lived in the home of a prophet?"

I tried to smile, but a tear melted down my cheek. I nuzzled my head into her shoulder and said, "Yes, Mama." I wished down deep in my bones that I could feel as brave inside as I was trying to be.

Suddenly Phillipe ran through the door. "Look, someone's coming." Everyone filed out to the yard. There, just turning onto our road was Brother Joseph, but he wasn't alone. From where I was standing I counted eight men with him. When he pulled the wagon to a stop, Ren came up scratching his head.

"Sister Saunders!" Joseph shouted from his wagon. "I found these gentlemen with nothing to do on this fine day. And you know what they say about idle hands." Everyone laughed. "I'd like your permission to put them to work."

The men began pulling tools out of the wagon. Joseph jumped down to join them. Then slapping Ren on the back he said, "Let's see if we can't get your family some breathing space."

CHAPTER FIVE

A New Friend

I sat cross-legged on the rug near the fireplace. Julia's chubby hands clapped together each time I lifted my fingers from over my eyes.

"I see you," I said in the sing-song voice she loved. Little Joseph pulled himself up to standing by gripping my shoulder. I slid my arm around him and swung him gently into my lap. He rubbed his eyes and yawned big. "You're a tired boy," I said, rubbing his back. Emma smiled at us from the window seat where she sat stitching another gown for the babies.

By mid-December, it had been nearly a month since I left my home to come here. Though I missed my family terribly at first, we'd visited them once already. That made it easier. Brother Joseph's promise to take me home to visit as often as he could gave me something to look forward to.

He was away a lot, as Emma had said, but when Joseph was home the house bustled with excitement. Emma hummed about her work and he was always stealing up on us to swing a baby into his arms or to help with a chore. By day, he worked upstairs with a few other men on the Bible translation.* In the evenings we sat by the fire and listened to readings and stories from the Book of Mormon. Brother Joseph always seemed to know when I didn't understand something, and without my saying a word he would explain the verses clearly to me. I envied the babies for having their father with them.

Little Joseph's eyes batted closed, while I sat stroking his hair. Julia was already asleep with her head on my knee. Emma whispered, "I'll take her." I nodded, and we tiptoed up the stairs and tucked the babies in their beds.

Every day Sister Johnson agreed to keep an ear out for the babies so that Emma and I could take a walk. Today Emma wanted to finish her sewing, so I went out alone. Snow was just starting to fall as I walked down the lane.

I thought of my family in their tiny little hut. The Johnson home was a big beautiful house with lots of doors, windows, and fireplaces. Outside grew every kind of tree and bush imaginable. The grounds were large and all the sheds and barns belonged to them too. I figured a dozen families could live like kings here.

Walking down the road I pulled my shawl tighter

around my shoulders, when a burst of laughter broke the quiet. I turned just in time to take a soft, powdery snowball square in the face. Sputtering and brushing the ice off my eyes, I caught sight of a boy about three inches taller than me running past.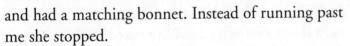

"You should've ducked," he said on his way by.

Then came a pretty girl in a beautiful red coat. It was trimmed with black and had a matching bonnet. Instead of running past me she stopped.

"Oh dear," she said, "I'm so sorry! You aren't hurt, are you?"

"No. I'm fine," I said. "Just cold." She began brushing the snow from my shoulders and hair. She looked about my own age, only more like a little lady. Her curls burst out from the edges of her bonnet like yellow ruffles around her face.

"I was chasing Lucas," she said, "but he's so fast, and my aim isn't very good. If Mother finds out about this, she will just faint." I thought of Cecile and smiled.

"Really," I said, "I'm all right." I looked down at my dress, thin and simple, and wondered how it felt to wear something as soft and warm as her coat looked.

"Forgive me. My name is Kathryn Hughes. But everyone calls me Katy." She curtsied and took my hand. "Lucas and I live up the road in the white house. I haven't seen you before. Have you just come to Hiram?"

I stood looking at her as if she were a doll in a store window. Even her cheeks were pink like the painted china faces. Everything about her was perfect, but what struck me most was that she seemed truly nice and honestly interested in me. Then realizing I was staring, I said, "Oh . . . well, I've been here about a month now. I live with the Smiths at the Johnson home. My name is Maren Saunders."

"I'm pleased to meet you, Maren. What a pretty name."

I felt color coming to my cheeks.

"The Smiths, did you say?" her eyebrows went up in surprise. "I've heard about them in town. They're Mormons aren't they?"

I nodded my head. I'd heard Sister Emma talking to Sister Johnson once about people in town who didn't like the Mormons. She said they'd run us out, if they could. I didn't understand why.

Now, I worried that Katy might feel that way too. I looked right into her eyes.

"Are you a Mormon?" she asked.

It was at that very minute that I realized how badly

I wanted to be. I wanted to hold my head up and say, "Yes, I am," but that would be lying. I fidgeted with the wool loops on my shawl trying to figure out what to say.

"No, not yet." I raised my chin. "But I'm going to be."

She looked puzzled, but to my surprise broke into a smile. She patted my arm and said, "That's all right, Maren. My mother says worshiping the Lord is a personal thing. It only makes one a better person. Anyway, I like you."

Until now I'd completely forgotten about her brother. He came running up and slid expertly to a stop right next to Katy.

"Lucas," Katy said, "I'd like you to meet my new friend, Maren."

"My pleasure," he said, bowing like a real gentleman. But as his head went down his hand came up and dropped a handful of snow down Katy's neck. She squealed and began hopping around like her dress was on fire. I couldn't help but laugh.

There in the winter cold I felt a flush of warmth come over me. Katy Hughes wanted to be my friend.

CHAPTER SIX

Peach Jam

Katy and I spent the next few weeks together, every free minute. As soon as her chores were done and breakfast over she'd bolt over to help me with my work. She said she didn't mind because her mother hardly ever let her help in the kitchen and never near the fireplace.

Today was baking day. Katy and I opened the  door to the oven with a large stick, then stepped back. The coals were deep red. Holding my hand to the side of the embers, I counted; one, two, three, four, five, six, seven, eight, nine, ten, eleven, twelve!"

Then jerking my hand out I said, "Sister Emma, it's ready."

Katy laughed. "I'm not brave enough to test the oven yet."

Sister Emma, bringing the bread pans over, said, "Good and hot girls?"

"Yes," I said. "I only got to twelve and my hand was nearly singed." Mama would have been so proud to think her own little daughter could not only tell the difference between a hot oven and a quick oven,* but could actually remove the coals, dust out the hot bricks,* and set the dough for baking.

Sister Emma always let me take home some of the bread we made, but it was hard not to be able to show my family the things I'd learned.

You see, a farmhouse and a sod house are nothing alike. Cooking over an open fire in the yard or in the corner of a sod house, as Mama does, is dirty business. Ashes and soot cover your clothes, skin, and hair. By the time you're finished, everything smells like smoke.

Here, each morning the ashes were swept away from the fireplace. On Wednesday mornings we even scrubbed the bricks clean. The smoke is forced up the chimney by a swinging door which closes the oven off completely. I'd never seen such a thing. Imagine! A baking spot right in the side of the fireplace wall.

Mealtime was faster and cleaner here too, and the food tasted so good I felt guilty eating it. But whenever I went home for a visit, I knew that the different ways my family and I were living now didn't change the way we felt. We love each other, ashes on or off.

"Katy," I said now, "I believe *your* baby is fussing."

"Oh yes," she said, pretending to look surprised, "I see you are right."

Each day, she and I took turns minding the twins. One day Julia would be "her baby" and little Joseph would be "mine." The next day we switched. It was a great game to pretend we were fine ladies of the city out airing* our children.

As much as I grew to love both of the babies, I had to admit I was becoming partial to little Joseph. I had worked so hard to make him like me, that now he wouldn't let me put him down. Brother Joseph joked that he only hoped the boy will learn to walk someday.

"Maren," Emma called, "Joseph will be back before nightfall. I think he'd enjoy some peach jam on this bread. It's on the left in the pantry. Bring some in, would you?"

"Yes ma'am," I said. Skipping around the corner I

 opened the pantry door. The shelves were lined with the summer's best colors: green beans, pink applesauce, orange, purple, and red preserves. There in one corner, just as Sister Emma had said, were six jars of orange-colored jam.

I grabbed one and hurried back to Sister Emma's side. She took the jar and after looking closer, said, "Oh, I believe this is apricot. The label is off. Joseph is so fond of peach." She held the jar out to me. "Would you mind? I know there's a peach in there somewhere."

For the first time in months I had that sick feeling in my stomach. Katy looked at me and nodded toward the kitchen. Feeling the jar, cold in my hand, I walked slowly back and knelt in front of the shelf. I sighed and picked up a different one. They all looked the same to me. I couldn't tell the difference. I turned one jar over and over in my hand. It had a label on it, all right. But as always, I had no idea what it said. Knowing the only way out was to guess, I chose as best I could. I held the new jar out to Sister Emma. In my mind I thought, please, let it be peach.

The minute I set it in her hand I knew I was wrong. She smiled, looking puzzled. Then as the realization came to her, she set the jar on the table. She *had* to know I couldn't read. I saw it on her face.

Before my thoughts untangled, I found myself running out in the snow. I had no idea where I was going, and I didn't care. The January air hit my face and I could feel warm tears turning cold as I ran.

A million thoughts raced around in my head. I hated being poor and worrying that there wasn't enough food back home. I hated sitting wrapped in a blanket while my clothes were washed and wearing them still damp because I only had one dress. I hated never knowing what was in a book or on a sign or in a fruit jar. It was as though people were talking behind my back and I could never quite hear what they were saying. I hated pretending I had a father like everyone else and feeling that my family wasn't real because I didn't. But most of all, I hated the feeling that there was a mess of secrets inside me that I couldn't let out for fear no one would like me anymore.

Somewhere off in the background, I heard a voice calling my name, but I hid myself in one corner of the big barn. There, I let myself cry every tear I'd ever fought back. It felt like hours, but I couldn't stop. Finally, sinking into the hay, I slept.

I awoke to the sound of someone moving near me. The cold air puffed around my face as I breathed. I sat up.

There in the other corner of the stall was Brother Joseph. He stood resting on one leg and plucking at a small bundle of straw. As I looked up at him he smiled and said, "This is probably the place I'd choose if I really wanted to be alone."

I didn't say anything. I felt small and embarrassed. I just looked down and picked at the seeds and straw that stuck to my dress.

"I saw you running past as I was tending to the horses," he said. "I went in and Emma explained to me what happened." He chuckled lightly. "Truth is, apricot would have been fine with me."

I could feel the blurring heat in my eyes again but didn't look up.

"Maren," he said softly, "it's all right. There are many people here, many of the Saints in fact, that can't read. Why, I myself have had very little schooling. My spelling and penmanship* are dreadful. In truth, that's why I use a scribe* as often as I do."

Still looking down, I shook my head. "It's different for you. You're the prophet."

"Yes. And lucky for all of us, the Lord looks upon the heart, not the learnedness of his people. We'll do no less here."

"What must Katy think?" I said softly.

"Katy's your friend. She loves you, as we all do. No lack of book learning will change that." He paused, waiting for me to look up. When I finally did, he was just standing there, smiling at me. Then he said, "I have an idea. Emma taught school for a while before we married. Perhaps she could teach you. We have many books here, and you'd be welcome to them.

45

When you feel ready, perhaps you could attend the school in town."

I couldn't believe my ears. Learn to read? Go to school? Even Ren had never been to a real school. It was too good to be true. I bit my upper lip to keep from grinning.

"Brother Joseph," I said, "I've no way to pay you for this."

"Maren, you're such a good girl. You work so hard to care for our babies. And the help you've been to my dear Emma... Well, I'm finding myself indebted to you."

We walked through the snow toward the house barely noticing the cold. Then, in a burst of truthfulness, I turned and blurted out, "He died, you know. My Papa. Two years ago last month."

Brother Joseph took my hand in his and patted it kindly. "I know," he said. "I know."

CHAPTER SEVEN

The Stranger

"I'm going to miss you M-A-R-E-N," Katy said.

"I'll miss you too, K-A-T-Y, but a week isn't so long, and I'll be B-A-C-K. I just hope my family remembers M-E. It's been so L-O-N-G."

For the last two months Sister Emma had taught morning lessons for Katy and I. Of course, Katy didn't need extra schooling, but she said it was better than staying home every day with Lucas.

Sister Emma was very pleased with how well I was learning. She said when a person wanted something as bad as I wanted to read and write, it wouldn't take long at all to learn. As hard as it had been, I hadn't told my family yet. Now, I was finally ready to surprise them by writing their names on a slate. Joseph had given me a primer* and I was nearly finished with it. Katy and I sang letters and spellings while we fed chickens, dressed the babies, or scraped dishes. We'd played a game for two days now where we had to spell some of our words as we talked. She was a lot better at it than I was.

Brother Joseph came in the door and held out his arm to me. "Are you ready to G-O?" I nodded. Then turning to Katy, he said, "Look in on Emma for me now and then, will you? With us both gone for a week, she's liable to be lonesome for some chatter."

Katy curtsied. "I will, sir. Good-bye, Maren," she said giving me a kiss on the cheek.

Outside, Brother Joseph lifted me up to the carriage seat. Sister Emma and Sister Johnson waved the babies' hands at us. Little Joseph cried and buried his face in his mother's shoulder. Then with a click to the horses, we were off. I waved until we rounded the curve in the road.

We drove steady for hours telling stories to each other and singing. About halfway, we stopped to water the horses. I climbed into the back of the wagon and slept awhile. Later, we ate the apple butter sandwiches Sister Emma had packed for us. When the sun got real low, the roads started looking more like home.

By the time we reached Aunt Elizabeth's road, I was sure I could get there faster if I jumped down and ran.

"Are you happy?" Brother Joseph asked, smiling down at me. He knew I was so excited I couldn't sit still.

"Umm hmmm," I nodded. Then as we turned down our path, I could see it. Little black curls of smoke rising above the tiny house. The sun was going down and left behind pink and purple streaks of light. It was so beautiful it took my breath away.

As I looked closer, there by the hawthorn bush was a horse. A gray I'd never seen before.

"Stop, Brother Joseph," I said. "Please stop."

He pulled the team to a halt and said, "What is it, Maren?"

"That horse. I think my uncle's come back!"

Not wanting to intrude on family reuniting, Brother Joseph dropped me off without coming in. He promised to be back on Friday, March 23rd.

From the moment I stepped through the door I felt something was strange. No one jumped up and threw their arms around me like they did the other times when I came home. Aunt Elizabeth stood stirring a pot over the fire and Cecile held Noelle in the rocker. Mama stroked Phillipe's hair, while he wimpered softly.

"Is he back? Is Uncle Riley home?" I asked, trying to figure out why no one would look at me.

"Maren," Aunt Elizabeth said wearily. "He's out back." She kept stirring but at least she glanced at me and tried to smile."

Though I'd never met him, he was my own Papa's brother. I could hardly wait to see him. Now Ren wouldn't have to work so hard to take care of us all. We had a man in the house again. Why was everyone so quiet?

I dropped my bags on the floor. "What's the matter?"

"Shhhh," Aunt Elizabeth said, as stomping sounds came up to the door.

There stood Uncle Riley, not quite as tall as I thought he'd be, but with Papa's same eyes and hair. I wanted to run to him but knew that wouldn't be polite, him just meeting me and all.

He grinned at me and said, "Well, well, you must be Maren. Come over here, girl, and say hello to your Uncle Riley."

I took a step toward him but something felt wrong. I was happy to meet him, but even though he looked like Papa, I could tell he was different. It made me a little scared.

I stopped in front of him and said, "Hello, Uncle Riley."

He grabbed my arm and pulled me closer. Then looking me up and down he said, "You look like you're doin' all right. Have they been feeding you up there at the Gardner place?"

Gardner's? I glanced over at Mama who shook her head ever so slightly. From the fear in everyone's eyes I guessed I needed to play along. I managed a "Yes, sir" before he let go of my arm.

"Where's Ren?" I asked quietly.

Uncle Riley's grin faded. "He's gone."

"Where?" I felt things would be more right if Ren was standing here.

"I told him no kin of mine was working for no Mormon," Uncle Riley said. "He didn't see it my way, so I told him to get out. And none of you better have no dealings with them neither. Hear me?"

I swallowed hard and looked at Mama.

Turning from me, Uncle Riley said, "Lizzy, I couldn't catch that bird. Send one of the kids out after it before I starve to death."

Mama kept stroking Phillipe's hair, looking straight at me. Aunt Elizabeth nodded to my sister who got up slowly and headed out.

Bird? I thought. Chester? Hickory? Uncle Riley wanted to make dinner out of one of our settin' hens. We had plans for them. Didn't anyone tell him? Or didn't he care? Thinking of the parcels Sister Emma had wrapped for us just this morning I said, "Cecile, wait!"

Uncle Riley shot an irritated look at me. "Girl, we have had about as much talk over this as I can stand. Chickens is meant to be et' and I won't listen to any more blubberin'."

I ran to my burlap bag and brought it over to him. I forced myself to look happy saying, "Uncle Riley, how would you like some nice, fresh ham?"

I lay in bed beside Cecile. She whispered, "Well, that ham ain't gonna last forever. Maybe till Sunday. Then what? He's just gonna kill them. We'll never have a yard full now."

"He can't kill them if they're not here, can he?" I said.

"Where they gonna be?"

"We'll take them into the woods, out past the stream, and turn them loose. At least that way they won't end up in the stew pot."

"No, but it might get *us* in some hot water."

"Cecile?" I wanted to tell her my surprise so bad, I ached.

"What?"

"I can read. Sister Emma taught me, and when I get real good, I'm gonna teach you, too."

Cecile didn't say anything. I pictured her smiling in the darkness.

"Don't tell anyone, Maren," she said.

"But why? I thought you'd be happy."

She took a breath and let it out slowly. "I am. It's just that, well, you remember how sad Papa always was about not having much schooling? Well Uncle Riley is real touchy about it. I just don't think this is a good time to talk about reading."

"He's not much like Papa, is he?" I could feel my voice growing husky and my eyes starting to well up.

"Nope," she whispered.

"I guess I just thought it would be different."

Cecile took my hand, squeezed it and said, "Me too."

CHAPTER EIGHT

QUIET WITNESS

I got up when it was just turning light and got dressed. It had been a week since Brother Joseph had brought me home. I hoped he would come early and take me back. I didn't know how he'd do it, I just prayed he'd come.

Uncle Riley never let up on his hatred for Mormons. He'd settle back just fine, then start thinking about them and get all worked up again. I ached to be where I didn't have to be afraid of saying the wrong thing. He'd be furious to know that I had been living with the Smiths. So all week long we'd just kept calling them the Gardners.

I stepped out onto the porch. The wind blew snow in small drifts up around the yard. The sky was all pink with new morning.

Suddenly around the corner I heard someone running.

Then Uncle Riley's voice broke out. "Hey! You there! Stop! What do ya think you're doin'?"

There in the yard I watched Uncle Riley run down a man in dark clothes, jump at him, and catch him around the legs. The man hit the ground with a thud. I froze where I stood, as Uncle Riley wrestled with him. It didn't look to me like the man was even fighting back.

"What are you doin' prowling around my house?" Uncle Riley said.

I squinted to get a better look at who it was on the ground. My stomach churned when I saw that it was Brother Whitney, from the mercantile.* Beside him lay a small barrel like the one Sister Emma stored molasses in.

"Well?" Uncle Riley yelled. His one hand pinned Brother Whitney around the throat. The other he doubled into a fist.

Brother Whitney sputtered, trying to catch his breath. "Please, sir. I was just leaving some supplies for the family here. To help out some."

Uncle Riley stood and grabbed Brother Whitney by his coat collar and yanked him up to standing.

"This family don't need no help from the likes of you. Hear me?"

"Look," Brother Whitney said, pulling away from Uncle Riley's grasp, "we're only concerned because Sister Saunders and her family can't get into town in this weather."

Uncle Riley stepped forward right up to Brother Whitney's face. "What do you mean by 'Sister Saunders'?"

"Elizabeth Saunders has been a member for almost a year. Now If you'll just let me by, I'll be on my way."

Uncle Riley reached out and pushed Brother Whitney's shoulder from behind. "That's right Mormon, get off my land."

Brother Whitney turned, this time with anger in his eyes. "Sir, I don't know where you fit into all of this, but one thing you best be clear on. This is not your land." He turned and walked off toward the road.

I hurried back around the corner and stayed quiet hoping Uncle Riley wouldn't know I'd ever been there. As I stood trembling, I heard Uncle Riley curse and something heavy hit the frozen ground. A  few minutes later he rode by at a gallop. He never once turned to see me pressed against the side of the house, too afraid to move.

When he was well out of sight, I walked around back and found the smashed barrel and molasses running thick and useless in the snow.

"He ain't comin', girl," Uncle Riley said. "I saw to that."

My whole body shook hearing his gruff voice. I sat in the rocker, still dressed and ready should Brother Joseph come for me.

"What do you mean?" I asked, keeping my eyes on the floor.

"I mean," he said hotly, "how long did you think you could fool me? I know you been workin' for that Mormon devil, Joe Smith."

I stood and faced him. Then in a voice braver than my own, I said, "Uncle Riley, he's not a devil. He's the Lord's own prophet."

Uncle Riley's hand came up as if he was about to slap me. I clenched my eyes shut tight, but nothing happened. When I opened my eyes, Mama was standing next to me. She wore a look on her face I'd never seen before. Her lips were pressed in a thin line, and her eyes narrowed with anger. She held one finger up toward Uncle Riley.

"Riley Saunders," she said. "How dare you think to strike my child, your own brother's child, for saying what your hard old heart would never understand. Now, I'll tell you, too. And we'll just see if you'll hit me."

She stood there so lovely and small but with more power in her voice than Uncle Riley ever had in all his ravings. The room fairly shook as she said, "We've learned for ourselves. Joseph Smith is a prophet of the living God. Nothing you can say or do will change that."

Uncle Riley stood glaring but said nothing. Suddenly Cecile arose, her eyes red from crying. But instead of her low, quiet voice, she spoke like Mama, saying, "He is. He's a prophet."

Phillipe ran to Mama's side and clutched her dress. He spoke so low we could hardly hear him. "That's right."

Aunt Elizabeth who watched from across the room, stood. She held her head up bravely and looked right into his face. I thought she was going to speak, but she didn't have to. With strength gathered from Uncle Riley's silence, she slowly nodded her head, never once taking her eyes off of him.

My heart pounded in my chest till I thought it would burst out. And then, from deep down inside me I felt peaceful and warm. A smile spread across my face that I couldn't stop.

Uncle Riley growled like a cornered animal, then left the house, yanking the door closed with a bang.

CHAPTER NINE

Stars Through the Roof

I sat by the window watching the wind blow. I wondered what Brother Joseph had told Emma last night, when I didn't come back with him. The door opened.

"Come see what I brung you, Lizzy," Uncle Riley said. "It's right outside." Aunt Elizabeth followed him to the door, afraid to look. But as he threw the door open, there in the yard stood a wagon and two horses. The wagon was old, but the horses looked good.

"Some fool peddler came in to town figuring to beat me at cards. Well, I showed him. And he'll be out of business by morning. Yep. Now that we've got his wagon, I'm pulling us all out of this place. Away from these cursed Mormons. I figure Missouri, maybe."

Aunt Elizabeth looked over at Mama and whispered, "Missouri?"

"Riley," Aunt Elizabeth said, "you can't drag this family hundreds of miles in the dead of winter. Why, we'll all freeze to death. Think of the baby."

Uncle Riley swung around and glared her quiet. "Listen here, woman. I'm in charge of this family now and if I say we're moving, we are."

"But Riley," Aunt Elizabeth said, "we can't leave Kirtland now. The folks here have been so good to us."

"It's them that's been filling your heads full of Mormon poison. And I say we've had enough."

"You have never once tried to listen," Aunt Elizabeth said.

"I know foolishness when I hear it!"

"If just once you heard Brother Joseph preach . . ."

His fists were clenched tight and the veins on his neck stuck out like cords. I looked around fast for someplace to duck, when all of a sudden, Uncle Riley's hands went loose and his lips curled up in an ugly grin. I was more afraid of this face than the angry one.

"All right," he said calmly. "That's what we'll do. Lizzy, you collect some things together. We'll go see this preacher of yours." He laughed out loud. "I'm a fair man. Ain't I a fair man, Lizzy?"

Aunt Elizabeth didn't answer. She just stood there looking worried and rubbed her arms like she was cold.

"Maybe, just maybe, he can save my soul," Uncle Riley said.

I awoke with a start. It was still dark outside. I could see the stars through the cracks in the barn roof.

We had ridden all day and into the night to get to Sunday worship services. Uncle Riley found a farmer who let us sleep in his barn. Mama stayed behind with the little ones so Aunt Elizabeth, Uncle Riley, Cecile, and I were by ourselves.

I peered through the dark to the corner where Aunt Elizabeth and Uncle Riley had bedded down hours before. I could hear Cecile breathing deep. From my corner, it looked like Aunt Elizabeth was lying there all alone.

I crawled over to where the two horses were sleeping and quickly saw that one was missing. I shook Cecile's arm lightly. "Wake up," I whispered. "Uncle Riley's gone."

CHAPTER TEN

Daybreak

We rode the mile or so toward the Johnson farm in silence. Uncle Riley never tried to explain where he'd been all night. He kept saying that he was truly excited to hear Brother Joseph preach. Cecile and I sat in the back and just looked at each other. We didn't believe him.

My heart beat strong at the thought of seeing Sister Emma and the babies again. If Uncle Riley stayed in the mood he seemed to be in, maybe I could even see Katy and if need be, tell them all a proper good-bye.

My mind was still troubled with Uncle Riley's sudden change of heart. I nudged Cecile and whispered, "Why's he *really* letting us go to this meeting?" She shrugged her shoulders.

I thought how wonderful it would be if Brother Joseph could actually get through to Uncle Riley. Really though, I couldn't imagine him in the same room with Brother Joseph. Or my papa, come to think of it. How could brothers be so different?

By the time we pulled up behind the other wag-ons, dozens of people were already seated on benches in the front yard of the Johnson house. There wasn't enough room anywhere but outside for the hundreds of Saints to gather, so even in winter, Joseph usually spoke from the porch.

We sat in the back on the log benches. As I looked over the crowd, to my surprise, I spotted Katy two rows up with her whole family. She turned and saw me. Whispering something to her mother, she jumped up and came running back to our row. I stood and threw my arms around her.

"Maren," she said, "it's so wonderful to see you. I heard about your Uncle Riley. I'm happy for you. Will you still be coming back?"

I looked at the ground and said, "I don't know."

"So," Katy said, "how'd you hear about the trouble?"

"What trouble?" I asked.

"Maren, my father has been here all night. He says disagreeing with a man's religion is one thing but trying to kill him is another."

"Katy, what are you talking about?"

"Last night a mob of about fifty men came

through here and pulled Brother Joseph right out of his bed. They dragged him to the edge of the woods to kill him. At the last minute, they just tarred and feathered him and left him for dead."

"No!" I shook my head. Cecile, listening too, reached up and took my hand. Uncle Riley talked and laughed with some other men, not paying any mind to us.

"Father heard Sister Emma's screaming. He has stayed here all night helping to remove the tar. We don't think Brother Joseph will be speaking today. Father says we've come to show him that most folks in Hiram are decent, upright people who don't tolerate such behavior."

"I have to see Sister Emma."

"You can't, Maren," Katy said. "She's taken sick from fear and isn't seeing anyone."

"Who's caring for the babies?" I asked.

"The doctor is with them now. They've been suffering with measles since last Thursday. Little Joseph is the worst. During this whole ordeal he took a chill."

"Oh, Katy," I said. "He's so little. He could die!"

Aunt Elizabeth reached up and squeezed my hand. "Maren, I'm so sorry." Katy continued. "I'll talk to you again after the meeting. Mother wants me to come sit down."

I sunk to my seat feeling weak. Someone offered a prayer, which I barely heard. The door to the house opened and Brother Joseph stepped out.

My eyes blurred when I saw the burned skin on his face and hands. He looked tired and pale, but smiled as though everything was fine. His hair was dark and wet and I wondered how long it would be before his hair could be washed clean of the black pitch.*

I couldn't stop my chin from trembling. I loved him so much. What sort of man could do this to the prophet, I thought. He's always been so kind and gentle to everyone.

As Brother Joseph spoke, I took comfort in the sound of his voice. He talked about loving one another and of brotherly kindness. As he looked out at all of us, I couldn't see a trace of hatred or anger on his face. I felt calm and happy just to be near him again. I prayed that, somehow, Uncle Riley would hear and feel the same things we did.

I glanced over at Uncle Riley who still smiled strangely. Then I looked at Aunt Elizabeth. She was staring at Uncle Riley's feet, her bottom lip quivering. I caught her eye and mouthed, "What is it?" She just shook her head. Finally she motioned with one finger toward the ground. I didn't understand. Then as I looked down, it struck me. There on his dirty brown boots were large ugly streaks of black tar. Straw and dirt stuck to the sides and bottom in clumps. Cecile covered her mouth, looking pale.

I felt my breath coming in short painful bursts, as I realized Uncle Riley had been there. He was one of those men who had hurt Brother Joseph. Now I understood his grin. He was proud of what he had done, and I was ashamed to even know him.

The meeting ended and people began to rise. I stood and ran out past the crowd to where the horses were kept. I couldn't bear to be near my uncle.

As I rounded the fence, I heard my name. I wouldn't look back. I couldn't. But again I heard it. Coming up beside me on Brother Simons' black mare was Ren.

He slid down and I ran to him sobbing. "Ren, he's one of them. He's one of the mob that tried to kill Brother Joseph."

Ren pulled me back and made me look at him. "Is Brother Joseph all right?"

I nodded, wiping my eyes.

"I never thought he'd go this far," he said.

"Uncle Riley is nothing like Papa. I hate him. He says he's taking us all away. But I won't go!"

"I know all about that. Mama told me. That's why I came. I'm thinking I can help change his plans." He held up a brown piece of paper with some writing on it and took my hand. "Come on!" he said.

Cecile was first to see us coming, but Aunt Elizabeth and Uncle Riley turned when she cried out Ren's name.

"Well, well," Uncle Riley said, in a nasty voice, "looky here. If it ain't the boy. Come to see your prophet did ya? Well, he's a sight to see today, ain't he fellas?" At that the crowd of men Uncle Riley stood with burst into laughter.

I felt sick inside. Whatever this paper said, it couldn't erase Uncle Riley's hatred toward the Saints. It couldn't make it so I could come back to Joseph's house and help poor Emma with her sick babies. And it couldn't fix it so we could be baptized, like we all wanted.

"Maybe you've come to say good-bye to your sisters," Uncle Riley said. "We're leaving Tuesday at first light, and ain't nothing you can do about it. You just stay here with all your Bible thumping* friends."

"Well, Uncle Riley," Ren said, "you're right to leave. Aunt Elizabeth can decide for herself, but whether or not my family's going with you is another matter."

"They'll go where I say they'll go," Uncle Riley said, his voice getting louder.

By now everyone was quiet, watching Ren and Uncle Riley. No one moved. I didn't know how Ren could be so calm. I was starting to shake.

"I just picked up a wire from a Constable Pritchert in Westbrook," Ren said. "Seems you're quite a big man where he comes from. In fact he's so anxious to meet you he rode all night and should be here within the hour."

Uncle Riley's eyes grew big with rage, but he just stood still breathing heavy.

Aunt Elizabeth came up and faced Ren. "Let me see that telegram," she said.

"Are you sure?" Ren said.

She nodded. "I think I can live with the truth." She unfolded the paper. One eyebrow raised up sharply as she read.

I stood quiet, lookin' at all the people staring at us. On the other end of the crowd I caught sight of Brother Joseph. He winked at me and smiled. I felt goose bumps up and down my legs and knew some-how that everything was going to be all right.

Aunt Elizabeth turned to Uncle Riley and said, "It says here Riley, that you're wanted in three states for horse thieving. Is this true?"

Uncle Riley's face went red. "Why you . . . !" he said, coming at us like an angry bull. But just as he reached Ren, his fist raised high, it was caught in midair. There gripping Uncle Riley's arm was Brother Joseph.

"Not today brother," the Prophet said. His jaw tightened. Uncle Riley pulled back fiercely but he couldn't get free. "Brother Saunders," Joseph said, "it seems that you're being challenged to a race, and you've been given a thirty minute head start. If I were you, sir, I'd take it."

Leaning over, Ren whispered, "I believe they hang horse thieves in Ohio, Uncle Riley."

Nodding toward the road, Aunt Elizabeth said, "Missouri is that way, you scoundrel."

───◆───

We reached home a little after sundown. Mama had left two lanterns lit outside to guide us back and I could hardly wait to tell her the news. "Brother Joseph baptized Ren, Cecile, and me in the river right after Uncle Riley left. Aunt Elizabeth assured him that you'd approve."

Mama clapped her hand over her mouth and cried, "Oh, how I wish I'd been there."

"Don't worry," Ren said, "Brother Whitney says he'd be happy to attend to your baptism next week, if you'd like.

"But what about Uncle Riley?" Phillipe said. "What if he never comes back?"

Aunt Elizabeth took a deep breath. "Maybe he

never will. But it's high time he owned up to the choices he's made. As for us, we'll manage, like we always have."

Mama held Aunt Elizabeth's hand. "Will you be all right?"

"I'm a sturdy woman. I have my family. I have the gospel. Who could want more than that?"

"Well then, Maren," she said, "I think we're ready, if you'd like to begin."

I smiled, opened the beautiful brown Book of Mormon that Brother Joseph had given me, and read slowly:

"I Nephi, having been born of goodly parents . . ."

GLOSSARY

In Maren's own words:

airing (pg. 42) When a baby is taken outside for some nice, fresh air.

Bible thumping (pg. 67) Some of the preachers in Ohio and other places could get real worked up while giving their sermons. Sometimes they'd start yelling and banging on the pulpit or the Bible. Many folks called it Bible thumping.

Bible translation (pg. 36) The Lord inspired Brother Joseph to translate parts of the Bible. He corrected any mistakes, and added any missing words that had been lost or changed over time.

big house (pg. 26) The main house on the Morley farm where Isaac, or Father Morley, lives. Many people, including Brother Joseph, stayed there.

disc weight (pg. 6) The metal stone used on one side of a scale to measure the exact amount of something like sugar or cornmeal.

foolscap (pg. 11) The most common paper we could get was called foolscap.

hand (pg. 23) Someone hired to work on a farm or ranch.

hemp (pg. 1) A strong, coarse rope.

hot bricks (pg. 41) The bottom of the oven is filled with red coals and stoked to a blaze. Then the embers are shoveled out and the hot bricks swept clean. Bread dough could then be baked right on the hot bricks, or in a bread pan.

in kind (pg. 21) When money is scarce, some people trade services for goods or trade one thing for another. Cecile could sew a dress for Sister Johnson, and she might give Cecile a ham for payment.

johnnycakes (pg. 30) One of the most common foods we had. It is a lot like cornbread.

ma pauvre petite choute (pg. 9) A French phrase used to mean "my poor little sweetheart."

ma petite lapin (pg. 33) A French phrase meaning "my little bunny."

makeshift pulpit (pg. 20) When a real pulpit is not available, the people make something for the speaker to stand behind, such as a table turned on its side or a large crate.

mercantile (pg. 55) A store or shop.

oven (pg. 41) Testing the temperature of the oven is tricky business. We open the oven door and hold our hand close to the embers, then start counting. Whatever number we reach before our hand gets singed, decides the temperature.

> Hot oven-12 seconds
> Quick oven-18 seconds
> Moderate oven-24 seconds
> Warm oven-30 seconds

penmanship (pg. 45) The way a person writes, or his handwriting.

pitch (pg. 65) Tar boiled down and softened enough to spread or pour. If it is put on someone's skin it could be hot enough to burn. When it cooled down it would be so hard to scrape off that it sometimes peeled the skin away too.

primer (pg. 47) The first and easiest book in a set of readers.

scribe (pg. 45) Someone who writes or takes notes for another person.

sod hut (pg. 26) A house make out of cut slabs of grass and dirt stacked like bricks.

waistcoat (pg. 27) A man's vest.

What Really Happened

On the night of March 24th, 1832, while Joseph and Emma Smith slept, a mob of fifty or sixty men broke into their home intent on taking the Prophet's life. He was dragged away and beaten, strangled, nearly poisoned, stripped, scratched, tarred and feathered, and finally left for dead.

Friends spent the remainder of the night scraping the tar from his body. The next morning he preached a sermon on brotherly love and charity to a congregation which included members of the mob. That afternoon he baptized three people.

Sadly, five days later, eleven-month-old baby Joseph, greatly weakened by measles, died from a cold and exposure to the night air. The Prophet Joseph, though still grieving the loss of his son, and recuperating himself, left on April 1st for Missouri to strengthen the Saints.

About the Author

Launi K. Anderson was raised in Los Angeles and San Diego, California. She worked for a large local bookstore for four years and became the children's book buyer. She loves historical fiction and enjoys the research as much as the writing.

Her favorite things are: Thanksgiving, flutes, autumn leaves, ballet, cats, and old photos.

Launi lives in Orem, Utah, with her husband, Devon, their three daughters, and two sons.